Beverly Lewis

Beverly Lewis Books for Young Readers

PICTURE BOOKS

Cows in the House
Annika's Secret Wish

THE CUL-DE-SAC KIDS

The Double Dabble Surprise
The Chicken Pox Panic
The Crazy Christmas Angel Mystery
No Grown-ups Allowed
Frog Power
The Mystery of Case D. Luc
The Stinky Sneakers Mystery
Pickle Pizza
Mailbox Mania
The Mudhole Mystery
Fiddlesticks
The Crabby Cat Caper
Tarantula Toes
Green Gravy
Backyard Bandit Mystery
Tree House Trouble
The Creepy Sleep-Over
The Great TV Turn-Off
Piggy Party
The Granny Game
Mystery Mutt
Big Bad Beans
The Upside-Down Day
The Midnight Mystery

Katie and Jake and the Haircut Mistake

THE CUL-DE-SAC KIDS

Tree House Trouble

Beverly Lewis

BETHANY HOUSE PUBLISHERS
MINNEAPOLIS, MINNESOTA 55438

Tree House Trouble
Copyright © 1998
Beverly Lewis

Cover illustration by Paul Turnbaugh
Text illustrations by Janet Huntington

All rights reserved. No part of this publication may be reproduced, stored in a retrieval system, or transmitted in any form or by any means—electronic, mechanical, photocopying, recording, or otherwise—without the prior written permission of the publisher and copyright owners.

Published by Bethany House Publishers
A Ministry of Bethany Fellowship International
11400 Hampshire Avenue South
Minneapolis, Minnesota 55438
www.bethanyhouse.com

Printed in the United States of America by
Bethany Press International, Minneapolis, Minnesota 55438

Library of Congress Cataloging-in-Publication Data

Lewis, Beverly, 1949–
    Tree house trouble / by Beverly Lewis.
        p. cm.—(The Cul-de-sac Kids ; 16)
    Summary: Abby and Stacy build a tree house and decide not to share it with the other Cul-de-sac Kids, even if they have to form a new all-girls club to get their way.
    ISBN 1–55661–987–1 (pbk.)
    [1. Tree houses—Fiction. 2. Clubs—Fiction. 3. Sharing—Fiction.] I. Title. II. Series: Lewis, Beverly, 1949–   Cul-de-sac kids ; 16.
PZ7.L58464To   1997
[Fic]—dc21
                                97–33884
                                    CIP
                                    AC

To
Leslie Brinkley
(Smile!)

THE CUL-DE-SAC KIDS

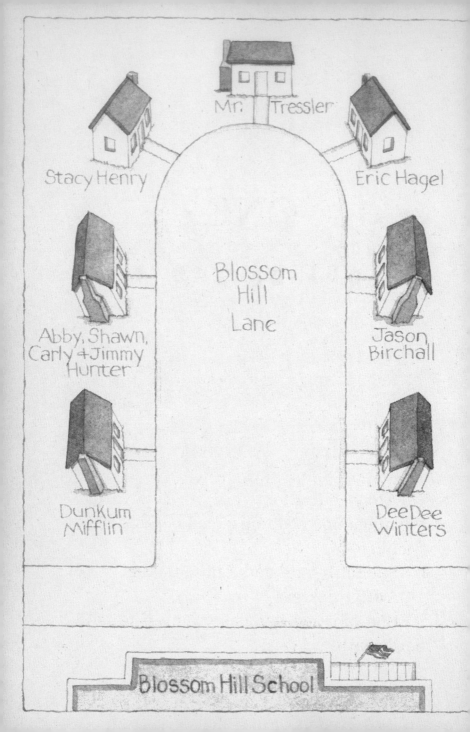

ONE

It was Arbor Day.

Abby Hunter tiptoed outside. She hid behind the backyard fence. She peeked through wooden boards. She watched Stacy Henry and her grandpa dig a hole. They were planting a tree.

Abby leaned on the fence, wishing. Wishing and snooping . . . on her own best friend.

Suddenly, she had a nose tickle.

A BIG tickle.

She pinched her nose tight. She held her breath.

Sneezing and snooping didn't mix.
She counted to ten in her head.
At last, the tickle went away.

Now Abby could snoop. Stacy and her grandpa were laughing and talking. They were having a double dabble good time.

Soon Abby had another nose tickle. But she would NOT sneeze. She would not let the terrible tickle win.

She twisted her nose. First this way, then that way.

She pooched her lips.

She held her breath.

Even pinched her nose shut with both hands. Of course, she'd need to breathe again. Pretty soon.

One quick breath, she thought.

She let go.

"Ah-h." She breathed in and out. But the tickle was still there.

Before she could clamp her nose shut . . .

"AH-CHOO-O-O!"

10

A sneeze escaped.

Stacy jumped. "Who's there?"

Abby tried to answer, but more tickles teased her nose.

"AR-GA-CHOO-O-O!"

There, she felt better. At least her nose did. But phooey! Stacy had caught her snooping.

"Need a tissue?" Stacy asked. She was leaning over the fence now, staring.

Quickly, Abby stood up. She brushed off her jeans. "I'm OK, thanks."

Stacy frowned. "What're you doing in the dirt?"

"Watching . . . uh, spying, I guess you'd say."

Stacy laughed out loud. "Why spy? Just come on over."

Abby felt silly. Snooping was stupid.

"Wanna help plant a teeny weeny tree?" Stacy asked.

"Thought you'd never ask." Abby jumped over the fence.

KER-PLOP! She landed on the other side. Stacy's side.

Of all the wonderful things God made, trees were tops. Abby liked trees. No . . . she *loved* them!

Tall trees, short trees.

Trees with flowers and trees without.

Trees with fat, wide arms. And trees with secret holes where squirrels hid nuts.

She especially liked the climbing trees. They had sturdy branches close to the ground.

Stacy's grandpa grinned a welcome. "Hi there, Abby." He carried the sapling toward her. "We could use an extra pair of hands."

Abby smiled. "Glad to help."

She noticed the tree's root system and its graceful branches. Beautiful.

"Ever plant a tree?" Stacy asked her.

"Nope," Abby said. "But I've always

wanted to." She helped dig the hole for the tree. Deep as can be.

She and Stacy steadied the sapling. Stacy's grandpa began to fill the hole with dirt. Lots of dirt.

Together, Abby and Stacy tugged on the long water hose. They watered the new tree.

When that was done, Stacy's grandpa stepped back. He tilted his head. First one way, then the other.

At last, he grinned. His dimples showed. "Fine and dandy," he said.

Stacy copied her grandpa. She took three giant steps back. She had to see if the tree was straight.

Abby giggled and did the same. Both girls eyeballed the tree. "It's real pretty," Abby said.

"It'll be huge someday," Stacy replied. "Like the one over there." She pointed to the oak in the corner of the yard.

Grandpa wiped his face. "It'll take

years for this sapling to grow giant-size."

"Our oak tree is big enough to live in, don't you think so?" Stacy asked Abby.

Abby stared up at the towering branches. They seemed to reach to heaven. Almost.

That's when her idea got started. A double dabble good idea.

"Let's build a tree house," she said.

Stacy's eyes shone. "Maybe Grandpa will help."

Abby looked up at the huge tree again. "I think we're gonna need a lot of help."

"Some of the boys might want to," suggested Stacy.

Abby wasn't so sure. She felt a little selfish. "Let's think about it. Don't say anything to the Cul-de-sac Kids yet."

"Why not?" Stacy asked.

"The tree house could be private," Abby whispered. "Just for you and me."

"You mean don't tell Eric or Dunkum? Not Dee Dee or Carly?" Stacy asked.

15

"Not my brothers, either. And especially not Jason," Abby said.

"You mean keep it a secret?" said Stacy.

"Wouldn't it be fun? *Our* secret?" Abby whispered.

Stacy finally agreed.

Abby could hardly wait to get started!

TWO

Abby headed for her own house.

She rushed into the garage. She borrowed two hammers and some long nails. She found two pairs of work gloves.

Her father was full of questions. "Are you making something?" he asked.

She glanced around. "A hideout," she whispered. "For Stacy and me."

Her father nodded. "Sounds like fun. Where?"

"In Stacy's backyard. But it's top secret," Abby said.

"What about your club motto?" he asked.

Abby didn't want to think about the motto. Not today. Not when she and Stacy were having such fun. Just the two of them.

" 'The Cul-de-sac Kids stick together,' " her father reminded her. He was frowning a little.

"What's wrong with one little secret?" she said. "Why can't we have a tree house for two?"

After all, she and the other kids on Blossom Hill Lane did everything together. Everything! Before school, after school. And most of the times—except for homework time—in between.

Two girls could build a tree house. They didn't have to share their plans, did they?

Besides, it wasn't really against club rules. Was it? She should know. She was president of the Cul-de-sac Kids.

18

If they *were* breaking the rules, nobody would know. Nobody at all.

★　★　★

Stacy's grandpa was a big help. He was strong. Cheerful too. He found scrap pieces of wood. And a bunch of lumber. Odds and ends.

Stacy's granny helped, too. She agreed to cover for the girls. She helped keep their secret when the doorbell rang.

Granny told them about it later. Jason and the other boys had dropped by. They were asking questions. Lots of them.

"We heard pounding," Jason had said.

"Where's Stacy . . . and Abby?" asked Dunkum.

Granny was double dabble good. She told them Stacy was busy. "And so is Abby," she said.

It was true. Granny would never lie.

But Eric wouldn't give up. He had to know if Abby was at Stacy's house.

Granny was so cool. She didn't let on. Not a single secret slipped out.

"Thanks, Granny," Stacy said. "You were terrific."

Next came a group hug.

"Hey, wait for me!" Grandpa hollered.

Abby and Stacy held out their arms. Grandpa squeezed into the hug. Now it was a BEAR hug!

Abby thought her ribs might pop.

Stacy squirmed and giggled.

When the hug was over, Abby giggled, too. A nervous laugh. "Our tree house is still top secret. Isn't it?"

"Sure is!" shouted Stacy.

But Abby was worried. *How long before the others find out?*

THREE

It was Saturday evening.

The tree house was finished. There were little wood slats for steps. A cute red roof on top. And plenty of room.

It was shaped like a box. A yellow one. High in the branches.

Abby and Stacy stared at their secret.

"We need stuff for our hideout," Abby said.

"You're right." Stacy ran to her house. She came back with her puppy, Sunday Funnies. "Every tree house needs a pet," Stacy said.

Abby agreed. "I'll get something, too. Our hideout needs to be cozy."

She ran home. She asked her mother for some old pillows. But Abby spoke softly so Sean and Jimmy and Carly wouldn't hear.

"Must you whisper?" Mother asked.

Abby replied, "It's a secret."

"Oh, a *secret*. Well, okay," said Mother, smiling.

Abby flew out the back door with two pillows.

She glanced around for snoopers. Quickly, she jumped over the backyard fence. Then she climbed the tree. Not a single Cul-de-sac Kid was in sight.

Stacy leaned out of the tree house. "Be careful," she called.

Abby did some fancy footwork. But she made it to the top. Inside, she arranged the pillows. "One for you. One for me."

"This is so much fun," Stacy squealed.

"Shh! We don't want anyone to hear us," Abby warned.

Stacy looked below. "Oops. I almost forgot."

They sat down in their tree house and grinned. "This is the coolest place on earth," Abby said.

"Sure is," said Stacy. Her puppy snuggled against her.

"Did you bring some dog food along?" asked Abby.

Stacy shook her head. "Why? We aren't spending the night."

"It would be exciting," Abby said. "Wanna?"

Stacy frowned. "Mom'll probably say no."

"Well," said Abby, "maybe we should ask."

"*You* ask," Stacy insisted. "It's your idea."

"OK!" Abby picked her way back down the tree.

Sleeping in a tree house was a double dabble good idea. Wasn't it?

★　★　★

"What did my mom say?" asked Stacy.

Abby pulled herself back into the tree house. She plopped down on her pillow and smiled. The wind blew through her hair.

"C'mon, tell me! What did she say?" Stacy asked again.

Abby crossed her legs. She grinned a sneaky smile. "You're allowed."

Stacy's eyes grew wide. "You're kidding! I can sleep outside? In the tree house?"

Abby could hardly believe it, either.

"How'd you do it? How'd you get my mom to say yes?"

"She said you could if *I* could," Abby explained.

"Really?" Stacy said.

"Your mom called my mom already," said Abby.

Stacy's mouth flew open. "Are you sure?"

"I'm NOT kidding," Abby answered. "But there is one problem." She paused for a second. "I forgot to tell her the tree house is a secret."

"Oh . . . no." Stacy groaned. "We'll probably be getting some visitors. Sooner or later."

"I know," Abby said. She felt rotten.

"We should've left things the way they were. Did we really have to sleep out here tonight?" Stacy said.

"Yes, we *really* did," Abby said.

Stacy glanced around. "Well, so far, so good."

"I don't see anyone," Abby added.

Stacy started to laugh. "We oughta have a watchdog. Sunday Funnies is the perfect choice."

Abby chuckled. "*That* ball of fluff?"

"You might be surprised," Stacy said. "My pup is amazing. Remember, he smells the funny papers three rooms away."

"But can he smell Jason or Dunkum?" Abby argued.

"Sunday Funnies can smell any Cul-de-sac Kid!" Stacy replied.

Abby kept her mouth shut. She wasn't going to ruin things. Because up here, up high was the very best place to be.

"Let's plan our sleep-over," Abby said.

"OK," said Stacy. "We each need sleeping bags."

"And a lantern," said Abby.

Stacy frowned. "Don't you mean a flashlight?"

"Oh, you're right. I've been reading too many prairie stories," said Abby.

Stacy nodded. "We each need a flashlight."

"We'll read scary stories out loud," Abby suggested.

Stacy shook her head. "Nothing scary. I'd rather tell secrets . . . until we fall asleep." Stacy leaned her head against her puppy.

"Do you really think we'll get any sleep?" Abby laughed.

"There's Sunday school tomorrow," Stacy said. "What if we fall asleep in church?"

Abby said, "We won't."

"Hope not," Stacy replied.

Abby wasn't worried about losing sleep. Or being tired at church. She was thinking about something else. How long before they'd have to share their secret?

She looked around. Their hideout was the best. It had little windows cut into the sides. And tiny flower boxes underneath. All theirs.

"What are you thinking about?" asked Stacy.

"Nothing much," Abby said.

"Let me guess—"

"You probably could," Abby said. "Is it wrong to keep this place a secret?"

"The Cul-de-sac Kids will find out," Stacy answered. "You know they will."

"That's what I'm afraid of," said Abby. "Maybe it's time for a new club. A different club."

"What sort of club?" Stacy asked.

"A girlfriends club," Abby stated. "A Best Friends Club!"

Stacy was smiling. She seemed to like the idea. "Starting when?"

"Right now," Abby answered.

She fluffed her pillows. A bird chirped outside the little window.

That's when they heard the sneeze.

"Uh-oh. Someone's spying on us," whispered Stacy.

"Better not be," Abby whispered back.

But somebody was.

Two somebodies!

FOUR

It was sunset.

"Don't move," Abby whispered. The girls hid under the tree house window.

Abby peeked out. She could only see shadows. "Sneezes come in threes," she whispered.

Stacy nodded. "I think you're right."

The girls waited and watched. One good sneeze deserved another. Especially in April when trees were budding. It was hay fever season.

Abby listened. Shouldn't be too hard to tell who was spying.

Then . . .

"Ah-h—!" Abby's nose tickle was back!

"Oh . . . don't *you* sneeze," Stacy pleaded.

Abby pinched her nose shut. "I'm trying not to." She held her breath.

But when she breathed, it sounded like "Aah-gah—"

Stacy covered her puppy's ears.

"CHOO-O-O!"

"We're toast," Stacy whispered.

Abby sneezed again.

From the ground, someone called, "Hey! Who's in that tree?" It sounded like Eric Hagel.

Abby grabbed Stacy's arm. They froze in place.

"I *know* someone's up there." This time it was Jason Birchall's voice.

The girls were silent as the sky.

Eric said, "Trees don't sneeze."

Abby almost giggled.

Then Jason made a weird sound. Like a frog or something.

That's when Sunday Funnies started barking. He wiggled away from Stacy. "Aarf! Aarf!" He leaned out over the tree house.

"Oh, *this* is great. Now the boys know it's us," Abby said. She heard footsteps running away. Were the boys scared?

"Sunday Funnies is a true watchdog." Stacy seemed proud of it.

Abby was upset. Stacy's pup had spoiled things. So had her own sneeze!

"Where'd they go?" Stacy said.

"Who knows," Abby replied.

Stacy sighed. "Sorry about my dog's big mouth."

"Don't say 'sorry.' *I* was the one who sneezed."

The girls grew quiet.

Then Stacy spoke up. "At least we kept our tree house a secret for a while."

"Only one hour." Abby felt sad, too.

Before Abby could say "Jack Sprat," the boys returned.

No sneezes now. Eric and Jason had brought flashlights. Giant-sized ones!

Abby ducked her head. "Lie down," she told Stacy.

But Sunday Funnies was too excited. He barked and barked.

Beams from the flashlights moved across the tree. Back and forth.

"Wow! Check it out," Jason said below. "That's a tree house and a half!"

"Stacy doesn't have a tree house," Eric insisted. "Does she?"

"Well, I'm not dreaming. Am I?" Jason laughed. "Let's have a closer look."

Abby bit her lip. What could they do?

Stacy whispered, "I think they're coming up."

Abby's heart sank. Their secret was history!

FIVE

"Private property!" shouted Abby.

Eric and Jason stopped in their tracks. "Says who?" Jason hollered. He was halfway up the tree.

Stacy stood up, hugging her puppy. "You're not invited," she said.

"And we're not kidding," Abby spouted.

Eric frowned. "How come? It's just us—Jason and me."

"We're *not* blind," Abby snapped. "We know who you are."

35

Jason shouted, "What's your problem, Abby Hunter?"

"Nothing," she said.

Eric tugged on Jason's shirt. "C'mon. Looks like a private tea party to me."

Abby felt funny. "Sorry, boys. We . . . uh . . . started a new club," she explained.

Jason and Eric were standing at the base of the tree. Their flashlights were still shining.

"What happened to the Cul-de-sac Kids club?" asked Eric.

"Yeah, what about *us*?" Jason said.

Abby swallowed hard. She didn't know what to say.

"We're having a sleep-over tonight," Stacy offered. "Just us girls."

Eric flicked off his flashlight. "C'mon, Jason, let's go."

Then Jason began to sing. "Nanny, nanny, boo-boo. We'll just have to sue you."

"Don't be silly," Abby spoke up. "You

can't sue us for having a sleep-over."

"We'll see what the *other* Cul-de-sac Kids say," Jason said.

"Yeah, we'll just see," said Eric.

Now Abby was worried.

But . . . wait. *She* was the president. The Cul-de-sac Kids couldn't do anything without her. Could they?

"Jason! Come back here," she called. "Don't cause trouble for the club."

"Me . . . cause trouble? Who're you kidding?" He turned and laughed. Then ran for the garden gate.

Stacy started climbing down the tree.

"Where are you going?" Abby said.

"We need sleeping bags, right?" Stacy asked.

"Some snack food, too," Abby replied. She followed her friend down.

"Hurry back," Stacy called and ran to her house.

"I won't be long," Abby promised, heading home.

What else could go wrong?

SIX

Abby was coming out of her bedroom.
Ka-poof! She bumped into her sister in
the hallway.

Carly stared at the sleeping bag.
"What's that for?" she asked.

"It's for sleeping," said Abby.

"Outside?" asked Carly.

"Where else?" Abby replied.

"Mommy!" Carly wailed.

Abby shook her head. When would her
sister grow up?

She hurried to the kitchen. The cookie
jar was full. Double dabble good! She

filled her backpack with goodies.

Two bags of crackers.

Some mild cheese.

Half a loaf of bread.

Peanut butter and jelly.

One plastic knife.

Four napkins (just in case).

A thermos of milk.

Two drinking straws.

Four oatmeal cookies.

And two apples.

She hurried to the door. Her sleeping bag was rolled up in one arm. Her backpack in the other.

Now she was ready.

But someone was coming toward the kitchen. She heard fingers snapping. And humming.

It was Shawn! She was sure of it.

Where could she hide?

Not the pantry. Too skinny.

Under the sink? Too crowded.

Behind the refrigerator? Too heavy.

Think fast! Could she make it to the back door?

Zip-p-p!

She flew past the fridge, sink, and pantry.

Whoosh!

She was gone. Outside.

Too close, she thought.

Relieved, Abby headed for the garden gate.

Squeak! The screen door opened behind her.

"That you, Abby?" It was Jimmy.

She turned to see her little brother. He was hanging out the door.

"Oh, hi." She faced him the best she could. Didn't want him to see her backpack, especially.

He stared at the sleeping bag. "Why . . . you . . . sleep outside?" he asked. His English was still jumbled up. Jimmy had been adopted, from Korea.

Abby looked at the sky. "It's a nice

night. Don't you think so?"

Jimmy peered up. "Yes, very nice." It sounded like *velly* nice.

Abby didn't mind. She just wanted him to go back inside. But she didn't say that. He might get too curious. "When you're older, you'll sleep outside, too," she told him.

"I old . . . NOW!" He came outside and stood up tall. "Jimmy Hunter very old."

Abby laughed. "First graders are NOT old," she said.

"Are too!" he insisted.

Now what? she wondered. She didn't want him to follow her. "Isn't Mom calling you?" she asked.

Jimmy cocked his head and listened. "Not hear mother."

"But you're hungry, right?" she tried again.

"I watch Abby put treats in bag." He pointed to her backpack.

The snoop!

"There's plenty more in the kitchen," she hinted.

Across the fence, Stacy was calling, "Abby! Hurry up!"

Abby felt trapped. "Time for supper," she told Jimmy. "Better go inside now."

But Jimmy was pushy. "I eat outside . . . with big sister."

He was being impossible. Definitely.

"I have to get going," Abby said. "Maybe some other time."

"NOW!" Jimmy stamped his foot. "Eat with sister now!"

Just then Shawn showed up. So did Carly. "What's going on?" Carly asked.

"It's nothing," Abby said.

"Is *something*!" Jimmy shouted.

"Well, Mom said to wash up," Carly bossed.

Abby kept quiet. She was tired of fussing.

Shawn spoke to Jimmy in Korean. Then they went inside.

But Carly stayed. "Where are you going, Abby?" she asked.

"To Stacy's."

"What for?" Carly asked.

"Mom knows, so it's okay," Abby said.

Carly squinted her eyes. "Why can't you tell *me*?"

"You don't need to know everything," said Abby.

"Better tell me!"

"I don't have to," Abby answered. "Good-bye." She hurried through the backyard gate. *Carly's such a pain*, she thought.

Abby was glad she had a best friend. And the new Best Friends Club!

She couldn't wait to get back to the tree house. The private clubhouse.

She dashed across Stacy's yard.

But . . .

Plop! She dropped her sleeping bag. It rolled down the slope. Abby reached for it, and the string came untied.

"What's taking so long?" Stacy asked. She was high atop the tree. In the wonderful tree house.

"Everything's going wrong," Abby muttered. She tied up her sleeping bag again.

"Did you see my sign?" Stacy leaned out of the tree house. She was pointing to something.

"What sign?" Abby turned to look.

"Down there," Stacy said. She was shining a flashlight.

Abby saw the sign. She read it aloud. " 'No Boys Allowed.' "

"Like it?" Stacy asked.

"It's double dabble good!" said Abby. She dragged her sleeping bag across the yard. Then she began to climb the tree. Partway up, a tickle hit her nose!

"Oh no. Not again," Abby complained.

"What?" Stacy called down from the tree house.

"I have to sneeze," Abby said.

44

"Don't drop your sleeping bag," Stacy said.

Abby couldn't stop the sneeze. "AH-H-CHOO!"

"Bless you" came a voice. A weird froggy voice. It didn't sound like Stacy. Not one bit.

"Oh, great," moaned Abby. "Guess who's back."

Stacy peeked out the tree house window. "Jason? What're you doing here?" she called to him.

"R-r-r-ribit," Jason's froggy voice replied.

Abby kept climbing. Faster.

Jason teased. "Well, look-ee there. Abby Hunter's playing Tarzan!"

Who-o-osh! Abby swung over to the tree house. She found Stacy's flashlight and turned it on.

Looking down, she saw Jason and Eric. They were standing at the bottom of the tree.

"You silly frog boy," she called to Jason.

Stacy agreed. "Hey, you're right. Jason does look like a frog. Especially at night." Stacy was laughing.

So was Abby. But the boys weren't.

Eric pointed to the sign. "What's this supposed to mean?"

Stacy smirked. "Exactly what it says."

Jason sneezed. Three times.

"God bless you," Abby repeated three times.

Eric spoke up. "Are you *really* starting up another club? Without the rest of us?"

"We haven't decided yet," Stacy said.

"Yes, we have," Abby replied. "Our club's already begun."

Jason chirped some froggy sounds. "We'll see about that," he said.

"We sure will," Eric added.

They left as quickly as they'd come.

"What was that all about?" Stacy asked Abby.

"I'm sure we'll find out," Abby said.

"Sooner or later," said Stacy.

Abby hoped it wouldn't be too soon. She was ready for a supper snack. And a cozy bed under the stars.

Without nose tickles.

SEVEN

It was past midnight.

Abby awoke with a tickle. A *foot* tickle!

She reached into her sleeping bag. Down . . . down . . . down. She scratched and scratched. Ah-h! Much better.

Soon she fell back to sleep.

Seconds later . . . another tickle. This time it was her elbow. She scratched it and snuggled down.

Another tickle tickled her. She must be dreaming. So she let the tickle go.

Soon it *really* tickled. Like a bunch of cooties!

In her sleepy fog, Abby thought of cooties. They had tickled her little sister
once. Cooties had ended up in Carly's hair.

Lice. That's what Mother had called
them.

Yuk! Abby shivered.

Now there were more tickles. Lots
more. Abby knew she wasn't dreaming!
She had to scratch the tickles away.

Quickly, she crawled out of her sleeping
bag. She started to scratch, but the tickles
were moving. These were very weird tickles. They were tickles that crawled!

She hoped they weren't lice. She
wanted to scream. But Stacy was sound
asleep. She didn't want to wake up her
friend.

Abby turned on her flashlight. She saw
the reason for the tickles. They weren't
lice. They were . . .

"Ants!" she hollered.

Stacy sat up and rubbed her eyes.
"Wh-a-at?"

"Look! We've got ants!" Abby said. She pointed to the little black dots. Crawling dots. Crawling black tickles.

Stacy leaped out of her sleeping bag. She did a little ant dance. "This is worse than a bad dream," she said.

Ants tickled the floor of the tree house. They crawled up the walls. And all over the windowsill. They even dotted the girls' pillows.

They were everywhere!

"I'm getting out of here," Abby said. She picked up her sleeping bag and shook it.

Stacy did, too.

The girls looked all around.

"We must've dropped food scraps," Abby said.

Stacy shined her flashlight around. "But I don't see any scraps. Just icky black ants!"

The girls tossed their sleeping bags to the ground. They scurried down the tree. Their sleep-over was over.

"See ya tomorrow," Stacy said. And she headed for her house.

"Bye!" Abby called and turned to go.

Suddenly, something caught her eye. A glass object—long and narrow. She went to the base of the tree. "An ant farm? What's it doing here?"

She noticed something strange. The ant farm had been tipped over.

"Who would do this?" she asked the darkness.

Then she knew.

Jason and Eric!

"Is this their idea of getting even?" Abby almost laughed. She was double dabble sure she was right. The boys were mad because they couldn't be in the new club. The Best Friends Club.

Silly boys. Their ant farm couldn't scare *her* away.

Nope! She knew what she must do.

Right away.

EIGHT

Abby hosed down the tree house with Stacy's garden hose.

Swoosh! She sprayed everything in sight.

Things got a bit soggy, except her sleeping bag. She put it on Stacy's back porch.

It was a warm night. The tree house would dry out fast.

Abby shook her sleeping bag again. She turned it inside out. She checked every corner. Still a few more ants. A few *dozen*!

She flicked the stray ants off with her

fingers. One . . . by . . . one. Just like cooties. *Yee-uck!*

Finally, the ants were gone.

Abby climbed back up to the tree house. She felt the wood floor. Still damp. She'd wait a little longer.

Then she spied the patio pillows in her backyard. They were waterproof. She decided to borrow them. Just for tonight.

Soon the pillows were laid out. She unrolled her sleeping bag on top of them. She couldn't wait to guard the hideout. She would sleep in the tree house. All by herself. Her very own tree house. At least for tonight.

★　★　★

When morning came, Abby peeked one eye open.

No more ants. All clear!

She rubbed her eyes and sat up.

Flump! Something soft tapped her head. She looked up. White strips of paper

54

floated above her. "Someone was very busy last night. I think I know who."

A toilet paper tent hung over the tree house. Like a huge spider web!

Abby laughed. "Wait'll Stacy sees this."

She got up and climbed down the tree. Stepping back, she looked at the oak tree. Her eyes scanned the huge trunk.

Then she saw it! Someone had marked out the word "boys" on Stacy's sign. Now it read: *No Girls Allowed.*

Abby frowned. "Wait'll Stacy sees *this*," she said.

Jason and Eric were acting like big babies. They had no right to spoil the sign!

She thought and thought. The boys were out very late last night.

Hm-m . . . She could get Jason and Eric in BIG trouble. All she'd have to do is tattle.

Should I? she wondered.

★　★　★

Abby stopped Stacy in the hall before Sunday school. "I think Jason and Eric decorated our tree house."

"I'm not surprised," Stacy said. "My mom saw it, too. But let's not tattle."

"Why not? They deserve it," Abby said.

"They deserve something else, too," Stacy replied.

"What?" asked Abby.

"I think you already know." Stacy turned to the classroom.

What's she mean? Abby wondered. She followed Stacy to Sunday school. The older Cul-de-sac Kids were already sitting down. Shawn, Abby's Korean brother, was grinning at her. So was Dunkum, the tallest boy on Blossom Hill Lane.

Jason and Eric were smiling, too.

Abby sat beside Stacy. "What's so funny?"

"Who knows. But we'd better be ready for anything," Stacy answered.

Just then a folded note landed on

Abby's lap. She opened it.

The note read: *Remember the CDS Kids' Motto?* Signed: *The CDS Boys*.

Abby handed the note to Stacy.

Stacy read it. "Looks like the boys are in this together."

Abby nodded. "No kidding."

Stacy pulled on her curls. "Shouldn't we share the tree house with them?"

Abby couldn't believe her ears. "Are you crazy?" she whispered. "No way!"

The teacher arrived. It was time to begin.

Stacy opened her Sunday school book. She stared at the lesson. "Look at this." She showed Abby. "It's about sharing."

Abby wasn't surprised. She'd read verses like this before. She looked over at Jason and Eric. They were still smiling. Big smiles.

Rats! They're grinning about the lesson, thought Abby. Well, they could just keep smiling. She wouldn't give up the tree house. Not yet!

NINE

It was after dinner. Abby dashed to the tree house.

Someone had removed all the toilet paper. *Probably Stacy's grandpa*, thought Abby.

Soon Shawn and Dunkum showed up. Eric and Jason, too.

"We're coming up! Ready or not!" Jason yelled.

"No way!" Abby shouted back. "Wrap me up in toilet paper if you want to. Cover me with black ants. I'm not giving up this tree house!"

Dunkum looked surprised. "Why not? The tree house is big enough for everyone."

Abby looked around her. Dunkum was right. The tree house *was* big. Still, she didn't want to share. "Stacy!" she called toward the house. "Stacy, come!"

Her friend ran out the back door. She stared at the boys. "What's going on now?" Stacy asked.

Jason spoke up. "We wanna have a meeting. In the tree house."

"But we *always* meet at Dunkum's," Stacy argued.

Jason didn't give up. "The tree house is better," he said. "And you know it!"

Stacy looked up at the old oak tree. "So . . . you like MY tree house?" she said.

Abby held her breath. Stacy had called the tree house *hers*!

Shawn, Abby's adopted brother, piped up. "Please, Stacy? We have very short meeting. Yes?"

Stacy looked over at Abby. And Abby felt funny. *Real* funny.

"It's time for something different." Jason was getting pushy.

Abby glared at him. "Different? Like last night?"

"What're you talking about?" Jason shot back.

"We had unwelcome guests. Little black crawling guests," Stacy spoke up. "The opposite of uncles!"

There was a gleam in Jason's eye. "So you had interesting company, huh? Oh, sorry about that."

Stacy groaned. "Those ants were everywhere, Jason Birchall! A nasty trick! And you are NOT sorry!"

Jason smirked. But not for long.

Abby spoke up. "Stacy and I need to have our meeting now." She wanted Stacy to climb up. She wanted to talk to her friend in private. In *their* tree house.

"It's time for ALL of us to meet,"

Dunkum insisted. "The Cul-de-sac Kids stick together. Remember?"

Abby was tired of hearing about the motto. She wished she'd never made it up. "Too bad," she said. "Stacy and I are starting our private meeting. So scram!"

No one moved.

Jason frowned. He pushed up his glasses. "You've had enough meetings, Abby. You guys had a sleep-over meeting last night."

"We're not guys. And, yep, we sure did," Abby said.

"See? You ARE having too many meetings!" Jason shouted.

Abby wouldn't argue. Not in front of the Cul-de-sac Kids. She looked at all of them. "Hey, where's Dee Dee?" she asked.

The kids turned to count one another.

"And what about Carly?" Stacy asked. "Where is *she*?"

"Carly and Dee Dee will show up. Sooner or later," Eric said.

"We can't meet without them," Stacy said.

"That is, IF we were going to," Abby added.

"Don't forget little Jimmy," Dunkum reminded them. "He's missing, too."

Abby thought about her little brother. Was Jimmy still eating dinner? "Who's gonna get Carly and Dee Dee and Jimmy?" she asked.

She hoped all of them would search. Then she and Stacy could have some peace. And a club meeting—the Best Friends Club meeting.

Shawn nodded. "I go find little sister and brother." He jumped over the gate.

Jason ran to find Dee Dee.

But Eric and Dunkum stayed. They didn't budge one inch.

Abby bit her lip. Things weren't working out.

Not the way she'd hoped.

TEN

Abby sat like a princess, high in the tree house. Her legs trailed over the edge. "Stacy and I *have* to talk," she insisted.

"So talk," Eric said. "We'll wait. We won't come charging up your tree house. We promise."

Quickly, Stacy climbed up. She flew into the tree house.

The girls whispered. "What should we do?" Abby asked.

"About the Best Friends Club?" Stacy said.

"Can't we have *two* clubs?" Abby said.

"I don't know," Stacy answered softly.

Abby felt sad. Really sad. She looked around. The tree house was just right. It was perfect for two girls.

"Don't you wanna be my best friend?" Abby asked.

"'Course I do," Stacy answered.

"Then . . . what about just you and me? Shouldn't we have the Best Friends Club anymore?" Abby held her breath.

Stacy looked away. "I wanna be your best friend. But—"

"But what?" Abby said.

"We're *all* best friends," Stacy whispered. "Aren't we?"

Abby glanced at the Cul-de-sac Kids. Dee Dee and Carly were standing with the boys now. Jimmy too.

But nobody was smiling. Not the kids on the ground looking up. Not the girls in the tree house looking down.

Stacy bit her lip. "I miss my *other* best friends."

Abby knew who those friends were. She wondered about the tree house. Nine kids was a lot for one hideout. How crowded would it be?

She thought some more. Sharing was a good thing. The Sunday school teacher said so. A double dabble good thing.

Still, Abby was stubborn. She cupped her hands over her mouth. "I'm president of the Cul-de-sac Kids!" she shouted.

The kids on the ground listened. Their eyes were wide.

"I'm going to say something. Something important," Abby said.

Now the kids looked eager. Dunkum and Jason were smiling.

"We are NOT having a meeting today. Everyone can just go home," Abby said.

Faces sagged. Especially Eric's. He looked mad.

"No Cul-de-sac Kids meeting today," Abby repeated.

Stacy touched her arm. "Why not?" she whispered.

Abby shook her head. "Tell them it's *our* tree house. Just ours. Please?"

"I'm sorry, Abby. I can't." Stacy got up and climbed down the tree.

Abby watched her go. She wanted to cry.

Below the tree house, eight kids made a huddle. Abby couldn't hear what they were saying. She didn't want to.

In a few minutes, the kids headed for the gate. Stacy too. They were laughing and talking.

Jason called over his shoulder, "Have a nice *private* meeting, Miss President." He chuckled.

Abby wished he'd bite his tongue. She wished someone would've said "Good-bye." Just one.

ELEVEN

Monday morning. Time for recess!
Abby ran to the swings.

"Did you hear the news?" Dee Dee
Winters asked.

Abby leaned against the swing.
"Nope."

Dee Dee couldn't wait to tell. "We've
got a new club president," she blabbed.

"You do?" Abby couldn't believe her
ears.

Dee Dee was grinning. "It's Stacy
Henry."

Abby was stunned. "When did this happen?"

"Yesterday afternoon," Dee Dee said.

Abby wondered how that could be. The past president had to be voted out first. Didn't she?

Dee Dee kept talking. "We got ourselves a cool president. Really cool."

Abby didn't want to hear more. She ran toward the soccer field. "Everybody hates me," she sobbed.

★ ★ ★

After school, the Cul-de-sac Kids walked home together. All but Abby.

Abby wanted to join them. But she didn't.

She thought about her best friend. *Stacy probably IS a cool president.* Just like Dee Dee said.

She looked both ways at the street. But she tried not to look straight ahead. The Cul-de-sac Kids were laughing. They were talking about the school day. She heard bits and pieces. . . .

Dunkum said he wanted to plant a fruit tree. "For Arbor Day," he said. "Like Stacy did."

"Better late than never," Stacy said.

Eric agreed and offered to help.

Dee Dee and Carly said they'd dig the hole. They giggled.

Jason wanted to taste the first ripe fruit. Shawn said he'd help him. And Jimmy would hang from the tree. Upside down.

But nobody said a word about Abby. Nothing.

"What about today's club meeting?" Dunkum said. He was walking next to Stacy.

"Wanna use my tree house?" Stacy said.

"Yes!" Dee Dee shouted. "I love our tree house meetings."

"We're having another meeting?" Carly said.

"Can I bring my frog?" Jason asked. He did a jig on the sidewalk. He croaked, "Rrr-ribit!"

The kids were laughing. Even Abby laughed before she caught herself. But no one heard her.

No one seemed to care.

Not even Stacy.

TWELVE

Abby felt left out. *Really* left out.

But it was her own fault. She knew it was.

She decided to do a little spying. It couldn't hurt anything. Could it?

She went to Stacy's backyard gate. Leaning down, she peeked through the boards. The Cul-de-sac Kids were perched high in the tree house.

She watched them closely. They were having a club meeting. Without her! There in the tree house with that fancy red roof. And those darling little windows.

She twisted the ends of her hair. The kids were saying their motto. Like they always did.

A big lump bunched up in her throat. She tried to swallow. But the lump wouldn't move.

She coughed. Still stuck.

She coughed again. No use.

Then she felt a familiar tickle. A nose tickle.

"I should've stayed inside," she muttered. Before she could hold her breath, the tickle grew.

It grew so big. It got so strong.

"ARRRGA-CHOOOOOO!"

The sneeze blew open the yard gate.

The Cul-de-sac Kids stared at her.

"Bless you," Stacy said.

Abby tried to say "Thank you." Instead, she sneezed again.

This time, Jason and Dunkum said, "God bless you."

On the third and loudest sneeze, all

73

the girls chimed in. "God bless you, Abby!" Carly and Dee Dee were giggling.

Someone started chanting the club motto. Jason and Stacy got it going. "The Cul-de-sac Kids stick together," they said. "The Cul-de-sac Kids stick together."

They kept saying it. Over and over.

When they stopped, Abby saw the new sign. *No Snobs Allowed*, the words spelled out.

Abby's nose tickle was gone. But her throat lump was back.

She swallowed hard. She wanted to talk to her friends. All eight of them. She wanted to tell them she wasn't a snob.

"I'm sorry," Abby blurted. "I was so selfish."

"You sure were!" Jason hollered.

"Hey, nobody's perfect," Carly said.

Stacy smiled but didn't say a word.

Eric waved at Abby. "Come up here! You gotta check out this tree house. It's the coolest place around."

Abby didn't say what she was thinking. *The coolest place is where my friends are*, she thought.

She climbed up the tree. She looked at her friends and took a deep breath. "The Cul-de-sac Kids stick together," she said.

Everyone was clapping.

Jason was jigging.

Abby squeezed in next to Stacy. "Are you really the new president?"

"Just till *you* came back," said Stacy.

"Oh," Abby said, smiling. "I get it."

"Look how much room there is," Dunkum said.

"Oodles," Abby replied. And she meant it.

"It's a double dabble good tree house!" shouted Jason.

"Definitely," said Abby with a smile.

THE CUL-DE-SAC KIDS SERIES

Don't miss #17!

THE CREEPY SLEEP-OVER

Dunkum Mifflin has finished reading his 25th book. It's Miss Hershey's yearly goal for her students. The reward is a sleep-over at the teacher's house.

Miss Hershey reads a poem—"The Raven"—at the sleep-over. Dunkum's frightened. He sees weird shadows and hears strange noises. What'll he do in the old mansion on the hill?

When Jason Birchall offers to help Dunkum overcome his fears, some wild and wacky things begin to happen!

About the Author

Beverly Lewis loves tree houses! She thinks they are the most secret place a kid can have. When she was young, she used to climb trees a lot. Her mother called her a "tomboy." Beverly didn't mind because it was true.

"The best part about a tree house is the privacy," says Beverly. "You can write, draw, and dream up there next to the sky. And nobody knows where you are!"

Beverly thanks her sister, Barbara, who suggested Jason Birchall's ant farm prank. She also appreciates her long-ago

Ruby Street pals in Pennsylvania, who first taught her to share. "Without my childhood friends, there might never have been an Abby or a Stacy, Jason, or a boy named Dunkum," says Beverly.

Looking for laughs? Then read ALL the Cul-de-sac Kids books. You'll want to collect the whole series!

Learn more about Beverly and her books at *www.BeverlyLewis.com.*

Also by Beverly Lewis

GIRLS ONLY (GO!)
Youth Fiction

Dreams on Ice	*Reach for the Stars*
Only the Best	*Follow the Dream*
A Perfect Match	*Better Than Best*
Photo Perfect	

SUMMERHILL SECRETS
Youth Fiction

Whispers Down the Lane	*House of Secrets*
Secret in the Willows	*Echoes in the Wind*
Catch a Falling Star	*Hide Behind the Moon*
Night of the Fireflies	*Windows on the Hill*
A Cry in the Dark	*Shadows Beyond the Gate*

HOLLY'S HEART
Youth Fiction

Best Friend, Worst Enemy
Secret Summer Dreams

THE HERITAGE OF LANCASTER COUNTY
Adult Fiction

The Shunning   The Confession
The Reckoning

OTHER ADULT FICTION

The Postcard
The Crossroad

October Song

The Redemption of Sarah Cain

Sanctuary*

The Sunroom

*with David Lewis